9.95

Did you ever wonder if a cat understands what you say? Did a cat ever surprise you with a wise expression on his face that seemed to say, "I could tell *you* a thing or two... if I were in the mood to."

The boy in this story decides there are only two choices: either his cat does understand what people say or he doesn't. But these two choices lead to more and more choices, until something very surprising happens....

Perhaps you can think of other choices for the boy's cat. Or for his Mommy and Daddy. Put on your thinking cap, and come join the fun!

English translation and adaptation ©1983 by Larousse & Co., Inc.
DE DEUX CHOSES L'UNE ©1983 by Librairie Larousse, S.A., Paris.
All rights reserved. Printed in France.
No part of this publication may be reproduced, stored in a retrieval system, or transmitted in any form by any means, electronic or mechanical, photocopying, recording or otherwise, without the prior written permission of the publisher.

Library of Congress Cataloging in Publication Data
SEGUIN-FONTES, MARTHE.
    The Cat's Surprise.

    (A Larousse Thinking Cap Story)
    Translation of: DE DEUX CHOSES L'UNE.
    Summary: A child speculates on all the possible choices that would follow if a cat could understand what people say.
    [1.1 Decision-making-Fiction.   2. Cats-Fiction]
I. Beris, Sandra.   II. Title   III. Series.
PZ7.S4536 Cat   1983   [E]   83-54-33
ISBN: 0-88332-322-2
Adapted by Sandra Beris
Printed by Lazare-Ferry, Paris.
A Thinking Cap Book© is a trademark of Larousse & Co., Inc.

THE CAT'S SURPRISE

by Marthe Seguin-Fontes

Larousse & Co. • New York

I wonder if my cat
understands what people say.

I only have two choices.
Either he does or he doesn't.

If he doesn't, then I don't have to worry.

But if he does,
then he may hear Mommy say,
"Go put the sausage in the cupboard...."

Or maybe he won't be listening.

I hope he won't be listening!

Because if he hears about that sausage,
he'll only have two choices.

Either he will try to steal it...
or he won't.

There won't be any trouble
if he doesn't try to steal it.

But if he does,
he will snatch that sausage
and gobble it up!

And then Mommy may find out....

Or maybe she won't notice.
I hope she doesn't notice!

Because if she does,
she will only have two choices.
Either she will tell Daddy,
or she won't.

My cat will sure be lucky
if she doesn't tell Daddy!

But if she does,
then Daddy will have two choices.
Either he will laugh and say,
"What a silly cat...."

Or he'll get angry!

If he just laughs,
then we can all laugh too.

But if he gets angry, uh oh!

Either he will grab
my poor cat right away...
or he won't be able to catch him.

I'll be very happy

if he can't catch my cat!

But if he does,
he will have two choices.

Either he will scold my cat…

or he'll throw a slipper at him!

I won't mind *too* much if he only scolds my cat.

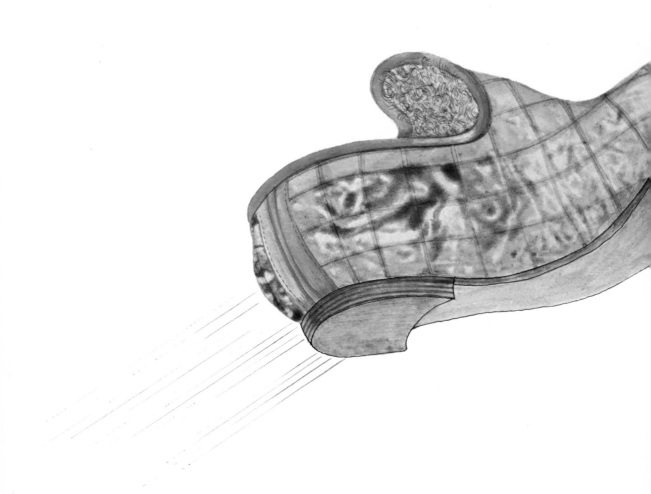

But if he throws a slipper at him,
my cat will get *so* angry,
that he'll leap up on the cupboard
and he'll shout,

By my tail and whiskers!
Only people could be rude enough
to keep a whole sausage
for themselves
and not share it!

When they hear my cat talk,
Mommy and Daddy will be too surprised
to answer!

But I will know…

that my cat understands
what people say!

EDUCATION